DEATH of the IRON HORSE

Also by Paul Goble

Custer's Last Battle
The Fetterman Fight
Lone Bull's Horse Raid
The Friendly Wolf
The Girl Who Loved Wild Horses
The Gift of the Sacred Dog
Star Boy
Buffalo Woman
The Great Race

Her Seven Brothers
Iktomi and the Boulder
Beyond the Ridge
Iktomi and the Berries
Dream Wolf
Iktomi and the Ducks
I Sing for the Animals
Iktomi and the Buffalo Skull
Crow Chief
Love Flute
The Lost Children

DEATH of the IRON HORSE

Story and illustrations by PAUL GOBLE

BRADBURY PRESS • NEW YORK

Library of Congress Cataloging-in-Publication Data
Goble, Paul. Death of the iron horse. Summary: In an act of
bravery and defiance against the white men encroaching on their
territory in 1867, a group of young Cheyenne braves derail and
raid a freight train. 1. Cheyenne Indians—History—Juvenile
fiction. [1. Cheyenne Indians—History—Fiction.   2. Indians of
North America—History—Fiction.   3. Railroads—History—
Fiction]   I. Title.
PZ7.G5384De   1986   [E]   85-28011   ISBN 0-02-737830-6

REFERENCES: George Bird Grinnell, THE FIGHTING
CHEYENNES, Charles Scribner's Sons, New York, 1915.
George E. Hyde, LIFE OF GEORGE BENT, University of
Oklahoma Press, Norman, 1968. Luther Standing Bear,
MY PEOPLE THE SIOUX, Houghton Mifflin Company,
New York, 1928. John Stands in Timber and Margot Liberty,
CHEYENNE MEMORIES, Yale University Press, New
Haven, 1967. Henry M. Stanley, MY EARLY TRAVELS
AND ADVENTURES IN NORTH AMERICA AND ASIA,
Vol. 1, Charles Scribner's Sons, New York, 1895.

for Keith

There have been many trains wrecked by Indian people in the pages of fiction, but it really happened only once. On August 7, 1867, a Union Pacific freight train was derailed by Cheyennes. The train was traveling from Omaha to Fort McPherson (North Platte, Nebraska), which was then as far as the track had been laid to join the East and West coasts of the nation. The tribes opposed the construction through their land.

The Civil War had recently ended, and the might of the army was turned to driving the Indians onto reservations. The unequal struggle was almost over.

The derailment was only a minor incident, but one that the Cheyenne people have remembered with pride and amusement. This book is loosely based on the incident. It tells a story of courage against the steam locomotive, a truly awesome and unknown invention of the white men. When Missouri riverboats had first been seen, they caused panic; tribes had fled at the mere rumor of the Fire Boat's approach.

Like everything else to do with war, the derailment had sad and unpleasant aspects. But from this distance in time, we can see that the Cheyennes were simply fighting for their lives, liberty, and their own pursuit of happiness.

Long ago, long before the white people ever came to this land, the Cheyenne Prophet, called Sweet Medicine, had a terrible dream: In his dream he saw strange hairy people coming from the East. There were more of them than buffaloes—as many, even, as the grasshoppers. They killed his people, and those few who were left alive were made to live in little square houses. And Sweet Medicine saw them kill all the buffaloes, so there was nothing left to eat, and the people starved. He saw the hairy people tear open our Mother, the earth, exposing her bones, and they bound her with iron bands. Even the birds and animals were afraid, and no longer spoke with people. It was a terrible dream, and they say that Sweet Medicine died of awful sadness not long afterward.

And then, one day, white people did come from the East. First a few came, and then more and more; they wanted all the land for themselves. Soldiers attacked and burned the tipi villages. They killed women and children, and drove off the horses. The people fought back bravely to protect themselves and to keep the land they loved. But they lived in fear. People said that those things which Sweet Medicine had foretold were surely coming true.

One day scouts galloped into camp, and told of something they called the Iron Horse:
"It is huge! It breathes out smoke and has the voice of Thunder. It is coming this way. The white men are making an iron road for it to go on. *Nothing* can stop the Iron Horse!" They tried to describe it. People had terrifying images in their minds.

Was it an enormous snake, or even an underwater monster which had crawled out of the river? Was this what Sweet Medicine had spoken about? Then there was even greater fear. In the minds of the children fear grew that the Iron Horse would suddenly come over the hill, right into camp.

Spotted Wolf, Porcupine, Red Wolf, Yellow Bull, Big Foot, Sleeping Rabbit, Wolf Tooth, and many others whose names are not now remembered, wanted to protect the people from the Iron Horse. They were not much older than boys, and knew they would have to be brave, even ready to die, like the warriors who had died defending the helpless ones.

"The soldiers have defeated us and
taken everything that we had, and
made us poor. We have no more time
to play games around camp. Let us go
and try to turn back this Iron Horse."
They left camp without telling anyone.

They rode all night and most of the next day, and came to a ridge overlooking the wide valley of the river. Thick black smoke was rising in the far distance.

"It is a grass fire," said one.

"No, the smoke has a strange shape. *Look!* The smoke is coming this way, *against the wind!*"

"Impossible," said another, "fire cannot go against the wind. . . ." But the smoke kept on coming, and underneath it something was growing larger.

"It is the Iron Horse; nothing else can make smoke go against the wind. See, it puffs and puffs like a white man's pipe."

When the Iron Horse had disappeared in the distance, the young men went on again.

"Let us see the trail it leaves," they said to each other. But nobody had ever seen anything like its tracks.

"These must surely be the iron bands binding our Mother, earth, which Sweet Medicine dreamed about. We must cut them apart and set her free."

With only tomahawks and knives it seemed an impossible task. But they dug down and chopped the ties in the middle, and hacked out spikes until the rails no longer joined together. The moon had long passed overhead when they finished.

Dawn was just showing when they saw
a small light over the level plain.
"Morning Star is rising," someone said.
"No," said another, "it is the eye of the
Iron Horse shining."
Those with the fastest horses galloped
up the track to find out.

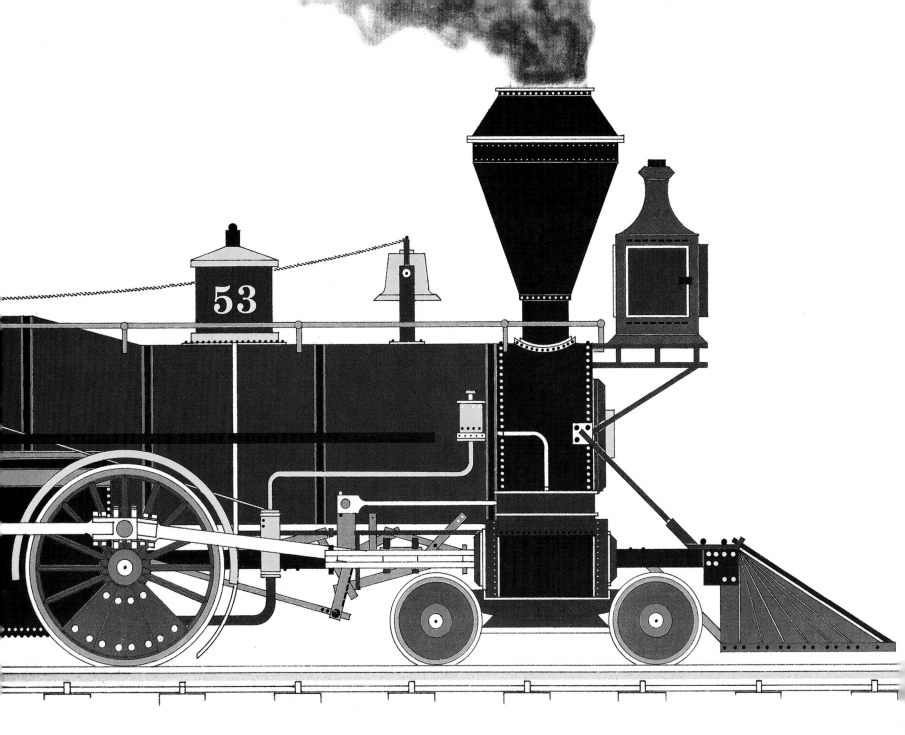

When they saw it was indeed the Iron Horse, they turned around, but their horses were not fast enough. The Iron Horse came up behind, huffing and panting, and belching out clouds of black smoke. It thundered alongside, sending forth screams and hissing and shooting sparks high into the air:
puff-a-puff-a-puff-a-puff-a-puff-a-puff-a-puff-a-puff-a-puff-a-puff-a-puff-a-puff-a-

The young men shot their arrows; one tried to throw a rope over the engine, but the horses were terrified and ran from the monster. Suddenly the locomotive jumped right into the air, and all the boxcars slammed and zigzagged together with a dreadful crash.

Everything was twisted up in clouds of dust and smoke and steam.
The dust blew away. The hissing steam faded. There was silence. One white man was on the ground; another was in the cab. They were both dead.

"The Iron Horse does not breathe any longer," someone said. The sun rose as they stood looking in bewilderment at what they had done. Suddenly a door in the caboose opened: a man jumped down and started running back up the track. He died full of arrows.

"Come on; let us see what white people carry in these wagons." They broke open the first car; inside was a jumble of broken boxes and barrels. The first box was filled with axes. Then everyone was hacking open cases, excited to see what was inside. They had never seen so many different things; they did not know what most of them were. But there were pans and kettles; china plates and glass vases; cups, files, and knives, like those which cost many buffalo robes in trade with the white men. Everyone found something useful. There were mountains of boxes: shoes, shirts, pants, jackets, tall black hats, and hats with ribbons and feathers. They scattered them everywhere. Best of all, there were soldiers' uniforms and blankets, and glasses which the soldier chiefs used for looking into the distance. They even found flags, and someone uncovered a beautiful shiny bugle.

In the caboose there were things to eat, and bottles of sweet juice. There was also a heavy tin box which would not open. They knocked off the lock; it was filled with bags of silver coins and bundles of little bits of green paper. The coins they took because the women knew to make holes in them and hang them on their dresses. But they threw the bits of green paper into the air and watched them blowing like leaves.

There were bolts of cloth in another boxcar; cloth of every color and pattern.

"Ha! Look at all this! Here is more than the stingy traders have! This is all ours! Look how much!"

"Well, this one is mine," someone said, and he ran off, holding onto an end while the cloth unrolled behind him. "I am taking this one," said another, and he jumped on his horse and galloped away with the cloth unfurling and floating after him like a long ribbon. And then everybody did it. When one tied an end to his pony's tail, others tried to step on the cloth, hoping to jerk him out of the saddle. They had great fun. The horses joined in the excitement, galloping this way and that over the prairie with the lengths of cloth sailing behind them. When they became old men they loved to laugh about that day . . .

It was only a smudge on the horizon, but first one, then another one stopped galloping to look.

"Another Iron Horse is coming. This time there will be soldiers with horses in the wagons."

They quickly gathered up all the precious things they could carry. And then someone said: "We will burn this and leave nothing for the soldiers." Taking red-hot coals out of the locomotive, they set the boxcars alight. They reached the high ridge and looked back. The valley was filled with smoke.

"Now our people need not fear the Iron Horse. We will make them glad when we give them all these things. Let's go."

This story has remembered the brave young men who defended their mothers and younger brothers and sisters from the Iron Horse. Whoever could have imagined that, almost within their lifetime, the Iron Horse would become the train on which we all ride?